ATTEMPTS AT A LIFE

ATTEMPTS AT A LIFE

DANIELLE DUTTON

Tarpaulin Sky Press
Saxtons River, Vermont
2007

Attempts at a Life
© 2007 Danielle Dutton

First edition, March 2007.
ISBN: 0-9779019-3-9
ISBN 13: 978-0-9779019-3-7
Printed and bound in the USA.
Library of Congress Control Number: 2006935538

Cover and book design by Christian Peet.
Text is in Fournier. Titles are in Nimbus Sans Novus.

Tarpaulin Sky Press
Saxtons River, Vermont
www.tarpaulinsky.com

Attempts at a Life is also available in a handbound edition.

For more information on Tarpaulin Sky Press perfectbound and
handbound editions, as well as information regarding distribution,
personal orders, and catalogue requests, please visit our website at
www.tarpaulinsky.com.

to my parents

CONTENTS

And it is necessary if you are to be really and truly alive it is necessary to be at once talking and listening, doing both things, not as if there were one thing, not as if they were two things, but doing them, well if you like, like the motor going inside and the car moving, they are part of the same thing.

~ Gertrude Stein

JANE EYRE

It started out I was hungry and smaller than most. Not pretty, but passable. Rest easy, for this is not another story about a girl and her father; I never even knew mine. I read a lot early in life, and seriously craved love, but was accused of being a liar by my only known family and sent away to learn to sell my soul to the Lord, and also to knit. Abandoned at school, I befriended an extraordinary girl who soon died like a martyr in a series of consumptive fits. Small but a natural watcher, I lived on through that season of death to learn to speak French and to draw. Eventually I wondered what existed beyond the fastened gate of my life. I wrote letters to newspapers and am so honest (not at all a lying sort) that I got myself a job in instruction and off I go. Up to this point I only had one pearl brooch. I had a black stuff dress. I might as well have been a Quaker!

•

At first much of my new life was what was missing from my old one, though still with chilly afternoons. I took long walks through generous woods and sometimes even on the roof to look at distant hills and (like all heroines, ever dissatisfied) to imagine what might be past them. I have a certain amount of palpable self-distrust as well as matter-of-factness, but stand in possession of a heartily romantic imagination replete with the usual voids and sprites and turbulent seas. With said faculties in tow I wandered the prodigious house becoming especially fond of the third floor, which was almost as solitary as I am, and rather like a ghost. Sometimes I heard laughter, not mine.

Eventually the master of the house, thus far a stranger to me, returned to show himself. One might assume the entrance of a rich stranger with a barrel chest would be just the piquancy my story lacked; yet his demeanor didn't send me rushing down "boisterous channels" of love. Although I went on in the normal way—walking dim halls—I was altered and alarmed. Meanwhile he began to summon me to his side nightly where I finally believed I could feel what I was born to do, feel, and be.

Yet perhaps I rush forth and relate too much, for he merely presented himself on the surface of things as a challenging conversationalist nights by the hearth as I calmly (or so he believed) worked on knitting. Some days he ignored me altogether. Yet, reader, I soon permitted myself to suspect he preferred my company to all other, even though I was small and poor. For I was considered by some to be almost a dwarf, although a pleasant one and rather with the air of a wood nymph. I thought: he wants to call me baby, but he is rich, melancholic, and much older than I.

So, to interrupt myself, I go to him and save his life one night and he grabs my wrist and almost does call me dearest and I say, stupidly, "I'm glad I was awake." I should mention there was one maid who was terrible at her job and only extended the stench of her life outward to the whole house (or so I thought at the time). He went away on a trip after that and when he returned he was done with me and I with him, which is that part so easily overlooked by gossipmongers. Perhaps I exaggerate! We ignored each other for a while is all. He was envious of my "heavy cloak of childhood," by which I mean my solitude. Apparently, he considered it composure. He wanted me to love him best and was even jealous of little girls. So he surrounded himself in a sea of shiny visitors to see if I'd drown on the shore with equipoise. He mocked me. Meanwhile, beneath my immovable hanging skirts he moved heavy breathing and hectic (of course he only dreamt about it). He saw the situation and he extended himself toward all the simultaneous possibilities for performance and concealment. He acted like a gypsy, a bride, a brooding dog, an eagle. Then he caught me on the other side of a door one evening and said, "I was in a room without light."

And it is done. It is love and it is (as he explained it) as though a string were tied from his lowest left rib to mine and would, upon separation of too many miles or months, bring forth wrenching internal bleeding, or death. A friend at last! Still, I palpitate at the sound of his voice more when he is harsh than when he calls me lily-flower or fairy, for I am neither beautiful nor given to dancing. In truth he was all I longed to be— adored, well-traveled, masculine. He was so in love he wanted to outfit me like a tropical bird instead of the plain (but refreshingly straightforward) English sparrow I might better resemble. I was forced to flee. It's not that I am silly so much as I recognize the gravity of life most profoundly. Would you believe, reader, that the chestnut tree in the near wood that I secretly held to symbolize our lovers' pact was cleft in two by a bolt of God's own lightning? Also, he was already matrimonially tied. That maid—in part—the stench wasn't hers but the wife's, who was demented. My master had kept her in a hidden sickroom for years. I fled for the sake of heaven and nearly perished from hunger and from my startled heart.

•

What followed was eventful yet boring in a way related to impatience. You see, after I recovered from an illness to do with wandering the countryside as a diminutive beggarperson, I managed to befriend folk known as the salt of the earth and to paint a fine portrait of an angelic young lady. She was prettier than I to be sure, but I know who I am. I also opened a school, found long-lost family members, inherited a bundle of money, redecorated a country house, and learned two foreign languages. So you see, I discovered my independence in the purifying aspects of my pastoral hideout, for there is nothing like the English countryside as regards the edification of a dissipated soul. Then one of my newfound cousins asked me to entrust my life to his. Thankfully I had a mystical hallucinatory episode, and so fled, again.

At last I recovered my lost love in a damp valley. Poor suffering soul! He was blind, but I think blindness is a cause for astonishment, so I returned to my master. He whispered, "I see all our tortures absolved in fog!" (His wife had jumped to her death off that very roof I once daydreamt upon.) We had babies then, and traveled the world by train, and I saw foreign landscapes through clear and unadulterated glass.

20C PASTORAL

We heard it all: hills sliding from yellow to green at a whim or a turn of breeze. Fish eating themselves in gutters. Birds laughing at us or else acting as missionaries among us, bringing bright plumage and fresh vocal arrangements of transistor radios. Today there's no use for descriptions of the past. But life changes on a dial, in a garden, a clinking of beetle wings, a shrimp bush and dry pink petals of chinese lanterns dangling. Once I thought: I'll just plant things until there's no time to be afraid. But storms are furious in their own way, green lightning and bullets as big as hail in the desert, as frogs.

My tongue reveals something faintly audible here. But birds come in off the low-slung roof and confess themselves atop cupboards. Even the occasional warm bird sandwich is prohibited. I spend a term untouched, living in an abandoned chophouse, pulling weeds. I post banns up and down the avenue, on palm trees and street signs. I drive a simple bargain. I ride my bicycle because it suits me to. They make me wear a W on my chest because they assume I'm working on a plan to make everything beautiful or watery or dark or light, but I don't even need to work at it. It was such a smooth transition—I nearly drowned one morning in water so clear I forgot I couldn't breathe it. But nothing's as easy as 1 2 3 and now it's our last breath and we'll take it in slow and steady. Is it? We need things: companions, games, meat. So we get married in the tribal sense. He will be able to listen and through a chink in some wall I'll be able to share my worries free from the epileptic shock of passersby. It'll be very convenient. Then this will happen then this will happen till now I'm an old lady. Poof.

Oh, and notice, I was talking about war, the burning of villages, all the reasons no one deserves the pity they want. It was just for laughs. Birds singing like trees, filling themselves like bare ruined choirs, so to speak, like worlds. But this is the moment when young flesh, when delicate young men turn out their own hearts deliberately, wistfully migrating towards me. Nothing of the sort, I tell them. I am not laughing. This is shame, the eye of shame. This is one big stupid century. It signifies: a bud, then nothing is left. It smokes for a while.

LANDSCAPES

1.

Here we have what is universally experienced as the most pleasant of landscapes: a sweep of field and cluster of tall trees; a small pond surrounded with fuzzy sorts of plants; then farther off, a village made almost entirely of stone chimneys and white smoke. Even the sky cooperates with us, its gray steeliness contrasting so forcefully with the vigorous greens.

The city skyline is a uniquely coveted tableau, especially when enjoyed from a high balcony with a lush park in the foreground. True, one must at times keep close watch on those friends whose moods are generally acknowledged to be lugubrious; otherwise, one can have few complaints against access to such a wide aerial vista, which can inspire pleasant dreams of unusual movement. There is something to be said, after all, for the energizing effects of the grid.

Here we see something altogether different. An abandoned mill puts one in mind of a sinister alien metropolis.

Beach scenes can, in and of themselves, be quite pretty, though one is constantly reminded of the inconvenience of sand. However, a wicker table and chairs with a pastel printed floral umbrella and plenty of cotton throws can quell any doubts as to the appropriateness of such a locale. Certainly the sound of the sea can be a balm to one's bruised soul.

2.

Joni looked up and asked her older brother to pass the rolls. He passed them. The next day he was nowhere to be found, nor the next, nor any day after. Everyone acted like he'd never been there at all.

3.

Eventually, I admit, I was forced to pick up the penny shining on the top step. It had been there for days and it was unquestionably not I who had dropped it. Who else could have been to this uppermost step? My concern was great, as you can imagine, for the penny was decidedly shiny, perhaps too shiny, suspiciously so. Having returned a third evening tired from a long day's work only to find it waiting, I felt I simply could not proceed under the false flag of happy ignorance. I would play the clown no longer! I bent and picked the penny up, turning it in my hand for some time, though it stubbornly yielded no hints as to its origin other than one small scratch on the side commonly referred to as the *head*. I remember it was the dinner hour and I could smell roasting garlic in the building next to my own. Do not think for a second that I slept that night. Oh no, I sat vigilantly in the dark till daybreak, my eyes pasted to the staircase leading to my front door. Unfortunately, nothing was to be learned through this particular act of vigilance, other than that there are indeed marsupials even in this part of the city.

4.

Josephine was silent for a moment. Then she replied shortly, "I've forgotten too."

"Oh, dear me! I'm sorry to hear that," said the literary gentleman in a shocked tone.

THE PORTRAIT OF A LADY

I was a tomboy and fought on open fields. The days passed unmarked and I called them: Mrs. Days. "She is a different child!" I heard the women say even as they were forgetting me. And while my sisters practiced their stitches in the parlor from the light of a beaded lamp, I stood on the battlefield with what I thought was a gun in my hand, but it turned out to be a bright green bird. Thankfully, an opportunity arose to chart well-charted republics. I sailed east in front of viewers. With body erect I sniffed the air, tilted generously with numerous impressions. Someone said: "If there is a wound then bacteria or peroxide will take care of it one way or another." I heard someone say: "Bring your body closer. Bring up your five parts." But I was the dancing girl for my own army after all, and a vixen.

Following various maneuvers of unperceived longing I was hit by friendly fire. With a faded silk backdrop they said: "Your particular brand of animation will be honored as we advance, blessed among nations of grandfathers, all dressed up." We rested together in courtyards, wriggling in short gasps, holding hands and shuffling towards dumb philosophies. We took trips to gardens to lie in the grass and ride the throb of our own barking language. I let them full blast into my glittering body. Yet I spent evenings fumbling in a universe of unceasing apprehension while they stared out at landscapes reflecting themselves: webs, censure, paved roads. In this way the years passed only at night and with them went my present face.

I was ill-suited to their diligent, glacial, grammatical ways. I had too many adjectives in my mode of parlance. In fact, they told me they were working on a way to move beyond verbal communication altogether. Fascinated by what they saw, they stood in front of mirrors. "How do you know what is attractive about you?" I asked. To which they replied: "Non-linear speech patterns are the shop windows of tomorrow." They loaned me books I never returned. I didn't even read them. Since the period of feverish kissing games I hadn't been able to keep up with their process of analyzing the black holes, knick-knacks, battlefields, etc. The books simply piled up on my body. I waited for months. I figured: Let them return and call me handsome as they see the great hump forming on my back. They did return again to tell me: "I was moved when I moved with you." It suited them to have me as intimate friend. Since they no longer knew how they evolved, they counted on me as genealogist and biological entrepreneur.

So I was once again made willingly, pleasantly, prototypically stimulated and wholly admiring of their reasonable world. They pinched my ass as they followed up stairs. But my rebellion against these so-called classical structures sprang continuous once I was remade as their tight-bottomed cheerleader. I knew accurate records would be necessary; I took photographs of the things I saw: broken contracts, joints, unknown regions of the body. Their forms were elegant in the slopes of my thighs, but flashes of recognition kept me ungenerous. They said they didn't have time for my questions and insisted my torso distracted them as it pertained to lingerie. The way I walked was too sharp. "Do I know anyone with such hair?" they demanded as I stood beside them in hallways. But I never really believed in my own involuntary animation until they asked me to coo softly while they slept. I said finally: "This machine of platinum and conquering does not suit me." I considered a move to another city but could never escape them since I put myself together out of what pleased them and have to carry my face like a mask. Then they caught wind of my camera, which they claimed did not record colors as they occurred. They said: "You are the assassin as well as the doomed man." They still don't have a word for me.

Now I'm a horse, a gun, an ebb. I'm listening for clues to their code. My research indicates that nearly every thinking person can come up with a slogan. What Has Been Done to Death Will Be Done Again. With my zillions of statistics I could attract the eye of any modern scholar, but I discard their paradise like chewing gum. I could have sworn there was something to this fight, something to do with the openness of the field. I walked many miles to get here, the dead middle of a summer afternoon.

VIRGINIA WOOLF'S APPENDIX

Evils of procrastination and cables & ropes & furs
& train oils, the human nose, a smack of Hamlet,
androgynous philanthropists. Scarcely readable by
merchant adventurers, scarcely in misty darkness of
decadence untranslatable to seafaring men and gifts
sent by King & Queen to Russia, i.e., "not commonly by seas frequented." The natural commodity
of God, helpful. Helpful to God for God behaved
Himself, a God indeed strung up canary birds rather
than monsters, monsters rather than women—for
the good of the Queen, the male & female lion, a
forest of chrysanthemums, a shop-window of gloves.
Yet judgment doubtless depends on a painting of
intimacy or one omitted uncle, a formal family, a
portrait of peers. The painting, omitted, the hostess
sobbing formally, the glass of water brought out while
children read Aeschylus in the garden: "Death and
cruelty hath taken hold of the crew in little companies
of ships, queer names rescued, flax and tallow down
below." Meanwhile the native word for *whale* comes
to Greenwich on unlucky passage. Whales engender

time. Men eat each other. Superstitious women spin a revolution favoring adult suffrage, flowers of speech, damask roses & trumpets & drums. But no moth was loosed upon the wallets of the poor, no orders drawn up by hobby-horses or dancers. The nature of the prize was silver whistles, immortal fame sprung from radish seeds, the best of Scott & the second-rate yacht of a fine, coherent nobleman. And the Queen's address was dull, a leaden circle of time ringing like a wooden lion howsoever she behaved herself, away like a water spout, strung up in a grove. The final cause takes no interest in facts: a forest of chrysanthemums, a shop-window of gloves. Re-impossible. To re-tell, impossible. Like a chapter from her cargo hold—dining alone, the safety of it rested on adventurers: "Adventurers All" or "Am I a Snob?" or "The Method of Henry James."

S&M

S says: "Roast the nuts for our breakfast, M."

Who thinks: I march like an army the dotted line blurs between me and many pure and beautiful things.

Says M replacing one coat of mascara with another: "There's a fly on the nose of the friar in that painting. Does the painting change if you consider the buzz of the bug?"

But she means to say there are strange noises in the pipes.

She used to make lists of names: Rose, Ruby, Claire. And for sons: Peter, Daniel, Thomas. The train to work is all subterranean walls lulling passengers to sleep in ties and handbags and mouths dropping open. There are other people she might have been, she remembers running to the opera once, she picked up a bug, it was cold out and the men in long tassels were yelling two minutes in front of tall doors. They'd been given the tickets by a friend with a permanent flu. He held her hand in the dark, it was her hand in his and then: people singing as they die and feathers. Everything is black and white in her fondest memories: the hanging gardens, the dappled asphalt. Or was that a movie with blond Italians and tennis?

Over dinner she says: "Running in the rain today I passed a fat, happy man with an accordion and heard a car crash behind me and it reminded me of you."

She means to say: I'd like to dig my teeth into the hard-packed earth until my gums bleed.

After sex she says: "These are the words you were always missing: sky, loft, music, dogs, pipes, puppets, war."

Although she too cried bitterly. And she revisits in her mind a rose garden and that smell that carried her nearly all the way to wherever it was back when things were breezy and it seemed nothing at all to say exactly what she meant. When it seemed nothing at all to write of butterflies and nudity all on one postcard and to speak freely of picking tomatoes under a wide-brimmed hat.

They stop in a shop. She is wearing high collars again, and heels.

Car lights like licorice whips slick the road outside the window in this weather and she is left with the sounds of dogs.

On the train to work a newspaper headline in the

aisle reports: Spanish Fisherman Drop Feet in Astonishment as British Troops Storm Beach Tuesday After One-Hundred Years of Wrong Turns.

She sits on the fifty-ninth floor and looks at the interstate and taps her fingernails on the glass. She writes a letter: What is it to walk away? Love treats my tongue like an oak leaf.

In the morning S says: "Hey, roast the nuts."

She says: "I am an army I march towards the shore."

And roasts the nuts.

EVERYBODY'S AUTOBIOGRAPHY, OR NINE ATTEMPTS AT A LIFE

ONE

My mother was born in 1901 in New York City. She called me Suzie. I must inform that I am not keen under that title. Early in my life I went to live abroad where the atmosphere was unsure and individuals assumed not merely positions but habitual blindness. This came soon after my integrities were pronounced ordinary by the crowding solitariness (i.e., America). I probed what might be called my life, my long life, with a strange fear of careers.

TWO

Born in Idaho in 1895, I broke through many cloth nappies before my mother had the good sense to send me off. Raised in an orphanage on the wrong side of town, still I learned all the classical notions and good writing. Thus, I embarked on the path of a newspaperman, which took me on fine adventures where the direct treatment of the thing was often called for. As regarding rhythm, I had absolutely none, not in the sort of sequence they usually mean. Instead, I spent my time reading about a kind of hallucinated trembling ancient Mayans used in a monotonous discipline involving telegrams. In this way I was rarely out of conflict with myself and wrote voluminous scented letters to my mother, though she could not read as far as I know, just spent her life working for United States Rubber until her demise in a diabolical event in 1909. That's what the orphanage informed me. I died in Italy in 1972, having purchased several luminous silver automobiles.

THREE

My seventh birthing resulted in one twin dead. The dead one I buried with yellow roses and the name Fanny. The living one we named Ivana; her first great feat of strength was to resist many offered hands of marriage and take up with a dancer from Cuba. She went to France circa 1930 to publish a small volume to considerable scandal. Whether or not one finds her work valid, she has come up as the darling of her time and proved that a series of sexual experiences can finally emerge as a kind of mathematics of the self.

Ivana died in 1939 farming organic vegetables in Tuscany with well-respected cubists. Soon after, my husband and I moved to Aspen, Colorado and began work on a distinctive national product, which he said typified the process of intelligence among clever people. However, that description seems to me now to more accurately define the efforts of an Englishwoman I knew, working around the same time, whose further-ance of the utterances of a generation are currently ingratiating themselves into a private mythology known mostly to the present editors of my daughter's selected poems.

FOUR

My husband was born 1887 in Germany after World War I. He moved to the U.S. and into my regular association after the others had come to N.Y.C. He was a purveyor of a kind of "magazine madness." Regular publication established him as too loud and erotic to claim his nativeness. His body was decked out with impossible objects to give the appearance of not so much a "German" as a "return home." His death by gas in Paris in 1927 was a high tragedy. I was lost *dans le métro* when it occurred.

My children are too numerous to be recounted in their entirety. My son Roland I found deserted on a beach after I'd left him there warbling with a bag of sweeties. You see, I was also so soft-hearted. My daughter Anasuya was born in 1922 in Chicago, moved to New York City circa 1943, and was a musician from her earliest memories. She loved dried cereals and was an innovative Buddhist training in elimination. Her eyes were marvelously vacuous and her pendulous breasts brought about several fistfights in foreign lands. She was always trying to "be discovered" south of the Equator, as she found North American men's gazes too slight to be satisfactory.

I was born in Mexico City in 1946 and spent my time reading of places with large orchids and strange, even sinister, fruits. Aware as I was that the sun was the source of all healing viruses as well as all danger, I resolved to live my life in unclean places—brothels, etc.—in an attempt to affect the orbital motion of the moon. It's too complicated to go into, but there are theories as to the purifying powers of this incandescent metal we call lust. I was considered a prophet by several of the city's acclaimed intellectuals.

In 1972 I traveled to Europe to ask the Ancient Greeks their thoughts on the permanency of heat, but was sidetracked purchasing several reproductions from a famous painter's later years and established myself in the capital of the world selling art to tourists with politesse for twenty dollars. I met a woman there who was born in N.Y.C. and lived in Paris during the late '20s where she made love to writers in a self-described "boring orgy." Her desire to retire from the bourgeois world into which she had been born made her great fun at sidewalk dances. In the mid '30s she left the city under the name Suzy Smith and, along with the editors of a famous literary magazine, fled to her death by continual suicide in London in 1950.

The places of my youth were places of deep passions.

I was born in South Bend, Indiana in 1905. My hair was molten, golden. I was interested in flight but was shot down over the hills as a fiery young maiden. I lived through a revolution in America once every fifteen years for most of my life. It's just as well. In a little while my life was shorter. I died in Germany in 1937. Just kidding, I'm from California. Of course there are large butterflies in California and birds with unusual claims to song. We once overheard a crane rouse us all to glory, though the unsightliness of the creature needs addressing: he stands over seven feet tall.

My mother was an American Original. We were raised among various Napoleons and Williams and told early what sex accomplished. In most cases, Greek tutors were told to rethink the Greek when we weren't around. As for cooking, I learned alongside the house-maid Amelia who baked an Italian grandmother's dessert involving berries of different vines and the dust of confectioner's sugar. Having learned through her, I was thus poised to place heartier desserts upon the sill. It's spelled dessert because you want more of it, whereas no one wants more desert. There's a painting of this in a grand museum: The Arab Man All He Has Is Sand.

Eventually, there was a gathering for my mother's funeral that involved the seizing of wetlands and the hat stand in the drawing room. What she left was an enormous house with white wooden parts and, to paraphrase the rest: kids that ran wild behind the veneer of that illustrious cliff overlooking the sea.

SEVEN

I was born in Socialist Vienna in 1934. The rain was steadily falling until my tenth birthday when my mother finally acknowledged my difficulties with Hebrew and sent me to a school in Israel to further my pronunciations. How I felt I had been exiled. I don't miss the rain. I live in a lighthouse off the coast of a Scottish isle and never mind the lack of company, though I tire of rereading whatever pamphlets and papers I find lying around. In the twilight the lighthouse becomes a flickering tongue flicking at the salt-water waves. I find it whispers the Hebrew words for *mother* and *bread.*

EIGHT

In the last two years of my life I had a major unfolding—both as male & female—and followed these orders through to their furthest logical conclusion: Broadway. It was a period of structural innovation in the American Musical and I was its brightest star. Along with my own first experiments in found movement, I traveled to Barcelona in '29 to visit with several accomplished image-making performers, whose visions in sun-related imagery seemed clear enough at the time.

NINE

I was born circa 1877 in Pennsylvania, and died in 1949. My own appraisal of my work is reasonable enough; the neglect of the housework was but one necessary offshoot of my root investigation into established circles. Interested in smashing things, I set the stage for every man to burst forth from the moulds that hold him in place. Eventually, I thought to reorder my house and get back to the comparative happy neglect of my earlier years. However, my declared intentions, when looking back, were too great a struggle in the endlessly viable series of experiments I enacted. And then something happened. I began to die from a nameless tropical thing related to heat and bacteria found in exotic bird droppings. I was buried on a July night in Rio. My daughters were in attendance singing a native rhythmic song, but my boys had all died years before me. My tombstone reads: "Dead century, where are your motley people, in Leipzig?" Each of my seventeen singing daughters placed a gray stone upon it.

ALICE JAMES

I am elaborately dressed like a bee for these outings and other young women also replicate fanciful works-of-nature: a lily, a pomegranate, a noodle. I sit and suck melon-flavored ices and swing my gloves over the edge of a white wicker chair. The scene is laid, the table, in the dining room. Father finishes the paper, a new one from France, printed on a special sort of material meant to be eaten after being read. He speaks: "There are useful cures these days for everything from a scalded head to getting tossed by a routine palpitation of the heart."

The following afternoon I meet a man in the piazza who is about my size, with small black eyes, a strong back, strong in the eyes and nerves. He is equal to the day, but Mother says, "I hope you did not try to stop him by the bridle." I request whether or not I should have rather thrown myself beneath his legs, but this she excuses with a nervous sort of laugh or really rather something of a brittle cough-cough. She's a splash of a social seeker and cooks elaborate meals out of pigeons to be later consumed by her patrician entourage with pocket-sized forks. There are hardly any great things to be said of her. But when I XXX she did not stop short. She grew to a colossus. The roles were reversed then and I was obliged to confess I could recall only little: "I dimly remember him doing it with his eye fixed upon a mirror." If only I had some new work to distract her: a broken engagement, a querulous sister.

Of course Father says scanty intellectual exercises are bad for my brains, indeed calamitous for the motoring power of my body and brains. "Dearest Doctor," I tell him, "If I am to learn how best *not* to abuse myself it seems certain I should close my stomach and my waxy neck to at least half-a-dozen of your books. There is no need to laugh beside my ear; we have all had in our life more books than we know what to do with." What a pity he considers me. I shall further inform you: about this time I acquired a passion for butterflies. With a homemade net of wire, broomstick, and cheesecloth I captured red admirals and great spangled fritillaries and the elusive morning cloak I sought near the shaded walk.

My other favorite pastime has been considered an unhandsome fixation. How feeble the parental instinct!

Here at the antediluvian verge of womanhood they once again insist upon primal innocence. "Is the door to the broom-closet a secret door?" my famously erudite cousin asks me. "If you think I do not see you, you are very wrong," I tell him. I sit on top of him in a paroxysm of mental and physical anguish. I say, "Ha traitor! If you loved me you wouldn't take the back door. My only escape from this Victorian mausoleum is your horse!"

Unquestionably, the overheated stimulations of this environment do little for me. Fed on prudence and undergrowth, who could ever expect much of me? I so admire people who say *damn*. I so like the act of bidding good night. An ordinary mail coach—even that brings relief! Lately I emerge from my silence only to brandish enthusiastically gesticulating hands at the Family Moderator who tells me, "They won't *stab* each other." And so we eat our dinners smiling. After all, as they tell me, one should have patience. Of course this gets me nowhere, which is to say, this gets me novelists for brothers.

PORTRAIT OF A WRITER
OF CHILDREN'S BOOKS

She was an ugly, shortsighted, affectionate little girl. She therefore observed animals closely. Some considered her pedestrian, earthbound, and lacking in imagination, but one time she put her toes in her privates.

She sits in the rocking chair on the front porch of the large white house and mouths off at the sky.

But even in those encoded journals one finds no hint of complaint, no guilty admissions. She simply went about recording her individuality in such a place. She made friends with rabbits and hedgehogs, minnows and jays, as one in solitary confinement will even befriend the mice.

SELECTIONS FROM
MADAME BOVARY

PART I, CHAPTER II

Night came: letter, rain, countryside, time. Charles turned. Emma hurried, stood. Inevitably house came weeping. For such she went, that's why.

Monsieur heard "what" "through" "lost" "to" "I" "I" "almost" "eat" "happens" "brace." His trees seemed him, himself.

Emma's *décolletages* twisted red. Partner-swaying to violinist's doorways, to pale low gentleman. Spanish curtain and violin. His relief opened to ears—the lives, the doctor's plates. Near turned to from. Out it woke, in yearning.

Down petered her *Corbeille* and the city came midnight. Girl Emma, pathetic sometimes, sometimes down. And everyone and ambitions (people) was further bourgeois. And she back under (arm blazing!), new from large alluring senses. In the highway. In the garden. To poke stuck waste, wept nights, was pregnant.

Polite morning in silent spent. A woman-like girl, her convalescence the tragedy. Noon wind weak moment to low "up" of sound (other bedroom blushed). Nurse the nothing. Nurse a peasant. Both went rapidly to hair that spent to weather, silently. There the dinner walls had nothing. Can nothing spot stopping? Boring—completely—Madame was there.

April arbor among moving young: candlesticks again raised emotion. Lestiboudois swinging above. Bovary muttered catechism. In ran dinner, furiously.

CHAPTER VII

One shrouded brought her and he to themselves, bare-headed. One fortune surrendered to enterprise: Léon. Beside actual—whether by passion (now A) and wearing history. Many would, usually sheet gray. The corner. He applying calmly cravat strings.

CHAPTER VIII

She *finis* came to the puffed-thumb Emma person. Provincial and jolly, wasn't square in the rattle. The rockets candle her, then collapse.

Rodolphe himself had had must the he the his he on come that on in ears (soft) a know was made. Horse and his ray out the firs follow in that into were and would between her. Again mustache spoke first: "Madonna on my grass, listen against velvet. Swelled of leaves, be distant." And him before was of sunrise. Fields fluttered his room.

Shipyards, tar, downstream of—stretched. They
followed oars, sang sailing. Small sitting black she
looked. Tell feel nothing. Chill spit.

CHAPTER VII

Close-fitting spineless love. Hearing hope crushed into pharmaceutical—gorged, crunched—his porcelain woman mistress. Sob, but not the gentle breast. Petticoat peasant thought of eyes on river as her story.

Memories talk, twitched (with velvet), walked, sighed, pacing (to the dead), returned, called, introduced, sagged loudly—once.

A cried candle stayed to water the sigh-wreath and pharmacist-things, to shock being for someone swollen to the bedsheets.

TWO STRANGE STORIES

ONE

It is a great pleasure. The wife and husband conduct suffering and then one does what he or she was doing and the other does what she or he was doing before. So he begins to do this one thing. It is natural to him. He says, "Rudeness comes rapidly from me." They attempt to (almost) simultaneously. This adventure leads her to believe that knowing very many things does not automatically yield an explanation.

The stranger arrives in the month of May. He says, "And so my business is inner balance." The husband recognizes an opportunity. He is in love with a woman named Ida in Connecticut. She is wicked. She urinates with birds and bees and violets and fishes. It makes one feel very likely that it is well to piss so. It is a happy time.

Meanwhile, the wife is seen in the city with a man who listens to her direct and moving pleasure, how she rises up and also how she never lets anybody say anything very naturally. She tells him she is a little hurt. We come to the epigrammatic part of it: a husband might not or may not even be in fashion at this point. It is natural that two men should be like that.

And so this brings up other things. These people are annoying. The husband and wife are cousins. Formerly they were married. By the time he gets to Connecticut he is a rich man. The stranger and the former wife act like perfect Americans.

TWO

A man shows up and sees a woman coming out of the station. She looks spiritless and jaded with artificial grief. He follows her on her way home with gray hope of ever being able to defile her. He cries out, "Wait a minute." He throws his leg over her and she says, "It's so uncomfortable like this." She looks the other way. He silently renews his vow to be the victim of inexorable pride. After considering this for a while the woman takes the lamp and moves down the hallway to the door he left open. He sits on her velvet sofa with her cat next to him. His own misfortunes press heavily against his thigh. The cat is forced to withdraw. The cat has energy enough to govern the world but just sits on a clump in the yard until a rabbit vanishes into some bushes.

HOW I MET MIKHAIL

My plan was to explore, in the essay, ideas of narrative via Hejinian's writing, which, according to Bernstein, "avoids closure in the pursuit of unfolding, multifaceted, restive thought," which unfolding is, I suppose, what often gives me the sense that her poetry performs a unique narrative act. I was in Russia at that time, staying outside St. Petersburg with a man who was no longer in love with his wife. I'd made his acquaintance a decade before on another trip, that one to Amsterdam. At the apex of a graceful bridge, I introduced myself. Or rather, I lied, saying, "I am Lyn Hejinian." He said, "I have heard of you and how you never end." We were both married, but I stayed with him in his attic apartment for several weeks, during which time I fell in love with a Dutch cookie: two thin round waffles stuck together with a delicate layer of maple-butter. What a wonderful treat! It quickly became my favorite cookie. In general, of course, I'm not one for favorites. I don't have a favorite movie or restaurant, for example, although I do have a favorite cheese—gruyere—a trait I share with Spinoza (my small dog), who also shares my love for lightly steamed broccoli and roasted chicken. Incidentally, when I mention Spinoza, she is here with me, but when I mention broccoli, broccoli is here instead. In this way, the movement of this story reminds me of what it was like to be read to as a child, especially when falling asleep, how there would seem to be beside me first a new blue jacket, then a wayward rabbit, an angry gardener, a pot of tea, one by one taking shape on the pillow beside me. Two years passed (after Russia), and quite unexpectedly, I ran into Mikhail again. This took place in Chicago in early December—the air was brittle, the sidewalks crowded, etc. When I returned to my hotel room I felt dirty, or the room felt dirty, though it was a pretty room, with hazy white curtains over an east-facing window. In fact, the room was very much like another room caught up with my memories of this man. The other room was smaller, though, and had an old-fashioned pedestal sink in one corner. Mikhail was making tea in the kitchen. I was washing my hair in the pedestal sink with a shampoo that smelled like lemon. My hair was longer than before and tucked neatly against my head with pins and combs not easily discernable to the casual observer; we'd just eaten a lunch of dates, almonds, goat cheese, and fresh-picked tomatoes. I put on jeans and a cotton blouse, and we sat together on a balcony overlooking the street. Mikhail began telling stories, one after another, each unfolding from the one before, until the sun finally set. By that point, of course, several key plot points had already been established. These mostly involved Mikhail and his soon-to-be ex-wife Margaret, an opera singer from Bristol; also a covert sojourn along the river; a dinner party with illustrious scientists; and an incident involving two ladies who have, by now, become integral to this story. Understandably, these developments brought about certain subtle shifts in my character (for example, I find I am unable to remove myself from this place, even with the help of the scientists). And yet, come morning, Mikhail will give me a modest present—something thoughtful, I think, and having nothing to do with the plot. We'll be on our way to the countryside to spend our vacation with friends; I'll open it on the train ride out of the city. It is a book. In it, I encounter myself on every page, but the me I meet is never the me I remember. It's me but me a misanthropic barber, me a German, a werewolf; or it's me but me advancing, me in slippers, me alone under a great gray sky. When we pull into the station, the people on the train stand and wave to friends or family. Mikhail stands in the aisle to get down our bags, and I see our friends on the platform waving to us beside all the waving strangers. What with so many words to be put together in response to odd kindnesses, Spinoza barking at birds outside, all kinds of routine behaviors, I find I have plenty to do. My thoughts now move toward spring. My thoughts are always moving, and sometimes they're moving with me, and sometimes they're moving with someone who is not me, the girl outside that shop, or the man in that boat.

A ROOM WITH A CORPSE

It is there on the floor.

"So, set fire to it," the man says bad-temperedly who I only this afternoon brought in from the night carrying that paper bag all crumpled and puppet-like in his shadowy hand.

"If you want to," I say, "I will leave it to you to do."

From the porch he follows me into a strikingly forlorn front garden with fat-rubbery plants and a high wall around it like a defense against cemetery intruders who probably have good reason to shout with all their shrewdness on top of this secret hill. Anyway, I am charmed at the possibility of being assassinated by fire-throwers! I look at my ex-husband with unresponsiveness too keen to show my suspicions. I sit down in a deep cradle of weeds below the dwelling's pitched roof. He taps on a window several times to call attention to the dining room, which is ruinous despite my furniture (which I lugged behind me all the way from a tremendous rough country). I reason he is a cruel agent of assassination and my senses nearly leave me, but then he asks, "Would you be glad about a cup of sour wine?" Even I have to admit this is big first-rate decorum.

I wait there until the late-hour. I am friendless and without a lamp. Having detected the falsity of his earlier offer of refreshment, I vow never to see him again. However, I soon apprehend his presence by the murmur of his not-far-distant voice. It seems highly improbable, yet I am forced to admit he is inside my house, talking with a Sister from the Holy Order of X. I hear the door as it's barred and watch through the filthy (locked) window as the two together begin to mount the steps, jerking to and fro, she with his assistance and he merciful to give it.

They have definitely stopped outside the bedroom door. I'm certain that together they're moving within a few yards of my bed, sitting or sipping tea under the eiderdown or within a few yards of my bed. I locate a piece of wood in the mostly empty grass and use it to break into my own dwelling with its cold linoleum and nothingness. How could they possibly know that today I would be the central character in a mystery of my own making? What motive was there? By now they've no doubt broken to smithereens the blue-veined china I tenderly packed and lugged behind me from a gloom thick with junipers.

Through the keyhole their faces are blurred, limp, satiny. He's done now, finishing up, buttoning. She will have traveled miles through the forest to become the person uttering there. Soon I apprehend murmurs of more civilized feelings: "My darling, my mud-spattered lover." But what has he even been doing here, pulled in from the dump, a nutcase? Through the keyhole could it possibly be he is perched upon my pile of rubbish in the corner, precariously bending over you?

Other hints I could give you, reader, which would be strong and dreadful. But tears are flowing from the now genuinely thankful nun's eyes and someone is shouting beyond the walls around my garden, invoking something, crying about: "Everything is left and left will turn queer!"

DREAM STORIES
(STARRING MICHAEL PEIRSON)

Every week Michael Peirson and I meet for coffee and go to the lake with our work. Waiting for us on the shore are two folding chairs and a red card table. We carry these with us into the lake. About thirty feet into the water we unfold and set down the table and chairs. The water comes up to the tops of our ankles. The reflection off the water gives us both a headache. When we go back to the shore, a born-again Christian tells us he is going to sue us because of the nasty things we said in front of his kids. We ask him what we said and he whispers, "Toilet."

DREAM

I was sleeping in my bed beside Michael Peirson. The sheets were folded and creased around us. I sat up and could see algebraic equations drawn in the air over the folds of the sheets. It had all been drawn with a white grease pencil. I realized that what I normally think of as the bed is not a bed. It was so obvious. I could hear the cat crying outside the closed bedroom door. I thought: I'm sleeping now but I'll wake up and I will never be happy after this.

Michael Peirson is getting married at a house in Italy.
The photographer is coming to take pictures of the
wedding party. I haven't started my period yet, so I
go down to the bathroom to wait for it. Then I dress
and go back to the family. Everyone complains about
my outfit. They insist I change. I go back to the bathroom and I still haven't started my period, but Michael
Peirson's sister has and she's left blood all over the
toilet. I try to wipe it away because everyone is going
to think it's my fault. When I rub it with a paper towel
it just smears over everything.

DREAM

Michael Peirson comes up to me in a crowded bar and tells me he loves me. We start kissing and that's when I remember the one quality about Michael Peirson I've always found off-putting: part of his tongue is detached; it just sits in his mouth like a piece of gum or candy. So I take the detached portion of tongue out of Michael Peirson's mouth with my own. I spit it into a napkin and show it to him.

DREAM

I am given a miniature horse to care for. I name the horse Michael Peirson. Everyone is sure I can't take care of him on my own. But I bring Michael Peirson to a small pool of water in a green valley. He drinks and is healthy and happy.

DREAM

We all travel by limousine to Michael Peirson's family estate in the country. I share a room with Michael Peirson. In the morning—the morning of the Winter Ball—Michael Peirson wakes early to be dressed by his maids. He returns to the room an hour later in a white gown with stacks of orange flowers in his arms. He sits on the bed so I can admire him. I'm still wearing my pajamas. Then I notice an old sliding glass door with a heavy wooden frame and thick glass. Outside is a small bay. The water of the bay comes almost to the door. The water is choppy and dark. The sun is bright, the sky is white, and all around the bay are hills of snow. There are icebergs floating on the water, rocking wildly like fake rocks made of papier-mâché. I say, "Look at this, Michael Peirson. A cloud is falling into the water." And sure enough, a small cloud, maybe twenty feet across, is falling out of the sky. It lands on the water with a slap. Then it starts to sink. As we watch, we notice polar bears cavorting on the snow-hills in pairs. I open the door and step out onto the snow. But the snow isn't even cold. It's like sand. I walk to the top of one of the hills and slide down the other side. I smile and tell Michael, "This is exactly what I wanted to do."

HESTER PRYNNE

I sit and watch a ship creak under its burden. Months
might pass until I hear that another has sunk, popping
from its fittings, flailing through darkness, breaking
up under cover of sea. But I have a daughter and she
is rare as anything. She is as seaweed is, jewels, birds,
groaning trees, storms, gold thread, moonlit fires.
Sometimes I'm not sure how she got here, but I don't
mean I'm not sure what I've done. She is my mirror.
I hold her up to me and cringe. This kingdom will
cover over with green mosses while straight-backed
trees look down. Life will be reordered out of joy and
an equality of sexual union. No one I know knows
calamity as I do. I think in the daylight as well as the
dark. My mind travels cities and villages. It follows
animal tracks to the perimeter and rests on its hind
legs waiting. Who is afraid of me? Even light runs
from me. I run after. In this way I run errands. But
I do not run from myself. I whisper into the fire at
night. Young boys watch from the edge of the trees
as I cook. Moving from the hearth to the table I'm
the flash of darkness between the cracks in the wood.
Soon the boys turn and scramble home, scratching

their cheeks on low branches. They fill themselves up on hearty grains and psalms. But they sleep poorly. They have dreams. The firelight is orange against the midnight of the ocean behind my home.

MARY CARMICHAEL

She dips down seven stone steps, not knowing where she's heading, but knowing she no longer need limit herself to dispassionate views and blank estimations. Here in the dimply anteroom she awaits a certain smoothing down, a packet of electrifying expressions, unusual liquors, the pug dog. Above her head an incensed tapestry waves just as people have noticed incensed tapestries waving for centuries; but she's never noticed one until tonight. She makes a line of startled indication at the woman in the corner, saying, "Reeling…'correct' rhyme, was it not quoted in the headnote?" but then rethinks, restates, "Your eyes are familiar and cast me in the role of previously established caller. Just so, just so. I am caught in a perpetual climaxing!"

(This morning Mary Carmichael beheld a soft eclipse, a snake, religious faith, madness, hyperbole, daggers, despair, wicked ceremonies, an upturned fire-engine, death. This afternoon she distinguished women in trains, mortgages, men with their heads willingly placed between crocodile jaws, snails, red and yellow tulips, flags, rivers, planes, war. Tonight, in addition to the tapestry, she sees she must attempt to cross uncrossable puddles, must face clarifying rejection, that sort of criticism, cliffs, etc.)

An elderly woman comes in to consider the problem and measure the dimensions of the room. In her hand she holds a pair of scissors; the two tips sparkle in the light of a single lamp and Mary understands that she must cut out her insatiable desire if she's to be free at all.

On her first attempt, Mary cuts a sturdy branch of black wood with pink specters of spring petals from a bookcase against the wall. Then she cuts a selection of Emily Dickinson's poems from a satin pillow on the floor. From a bright clay vase on a small wooden table she cuts silver-spangled stuff, but a fine Mexican parrot she leaves uncut in a glass paperweight the size of an overripe plum. Quickly, she uncovers a lobster in the slab, seventeen pairs of feet in the Turkish carpet under her own, a narrow man in a painting of a church, a wife in the door, two mysterious spheres in the wainscoting, a telescope in the mantle, a hymnal in a doorknob, and a communist in the closet. At last, and with a great sigh, she cuts a bright moon out of her own palm and a fly out of her ankle. The other ladies are impressed, as is the snorting pug. But Mary manages to silence them all by cutting a harlot out of the hat-stand and a queen out of the mat. Still their work is not done. They resume talking and talk long into the night.

At length, Mary suspects she's done all she can. She gathers up paper dolls, a roll of violets, her silk scarf, and a veiled hat cut from a fern in a pot. She wishes the ladies adieu, praising them for their beauty and human character, and they, in turn, insist on paying her for her work. Mary therefore retraces her steps without repetition (anteroom, tapestry, door), the coins imparting a provocative prospect in her pocket.

Back on the street, the night is strained, but clear and full of body parts, some brushing against her, some lingering in taxi-cabs or windows. Surprised to find the city so concentrated, and at such an hour, she makes her way over the longest bridge, at the apex of which she tosses her relics into the dilute conditions below. They make no sound when they hit the black water, though she imagines she sees chalk outlines of familiar forms appear on the surface, a split second, ablaze!

Minutes later, and up one flight of thin metal stairs, she finds herself in a wholly disreputable place (the currents flow through her, rush down her). She makes her request in a firm hand on the back of a matchbook and waits for the overseer to bring her her first assignation in a small room whose four walls are covered with astonishing paintings. In this place, in the briny light of a green-beaded lamp, Mary encounters two pirates and a sea-captain, finding only that her mind spreads. She undertakes a doorman, a cowhand, a machine-gunner, a Russian, Mr. Grey, St. Paul, a peevish Eddy, and all of Hyde Park—but she can't shake it. So she takes to screwing barmaids and ballerinas, one after the other, at the end of which procession she finds she's failed to gather herself together (as a character, in a fixed point), so she makes her way out of the establishment, back onto the street, slices a river out of a postbox and dives in.

Along the riverbank, munching on something of which there is blessedly more to be had in a steaming paper bag, she says aloud: I am I. Later, walking through Regent's Park, she steps over a snoring man asleep on the gravel path and finds herself opposite a statue of Achilles' head. It's here she chooses to slumber through the dawn, rising only when awoken by the spirit of some great good fun, and only then to boast of being slightly disoriented. Alas, she has no one to boast to but a small dun-colored bird hopping on the edge of her grassy bed. "O Bird," she says, "Do you know Aldous Huxley?" and together they watch a gray cloud rise over the ringing city.

Then the knitting of a moment, an everyday scenic effect—the morning air, the smell of bacon, the street-chatter beyond the twisting trees—forms an acute manifestation that allows her to become balanced in a poetic approach. With effort she remembers that she dined recently with a good many in view of pictur-esque landscapes, but she cannot recall if they were real ones. She recollects that, as a result of something someone said, she'd felt the need to freshen herself with a bit of looking-straight-at-things. "Had there been a quarrel?" she asks the birdie. "For one does get bored by such business. But how had I come to be taken with so much compressed meaning, vivacities, ignorant old women, clear phrases, and a burning need for one windy night of respite? Surely it was something more than a series of fluttering sensations over a dinner-party salver of veal?" As if in answer, the bird gathers wing to breast and trembles at the great desperate beginnings of it all.

SPRUNG

Once upon hard-pressed twiggy stuff, under spectacles of small trees, a gorgeous modern promiscuity made a pretty, rare bird. "With respect to your work," said the congregation of men at a useless festival under a hard-to-think sky, "Hey, death shaves me sideways, under an anarchy root. Just pull a thread so the world can worship the dictatorship of the warblers." Humming by the side of the cocooned road, the only familiar formulas were clear as all-at-once. All at once we shot the doctor in the back—his genius spinning and my triangulating heart, clear as compositions of nothing, but stunning. We are rooms rotting and dragged roots on concrete, magnificent confessions of nameless confusion and already quoted ideology, synonymous with slatternly houses, greenish in the back room. Both sides sway toward an edge. The line begins in the thematic pine-drift. There are manifestoes hiding under tables, but summer pavement breathes beneath the feet of giants failing. Dividing sermons hornlike at the river-edge, we tell where whispers melted and never never grew up. Come night the clouds bundle above the rest, past knowing just for me, to bear witness if only to a textured faith—voice or His Voice, a felt performance or break-you-apart. In favor of a sermon I cover an elder woman's limbs in the black orchard of river. She'd asked about failure, barrels of explosions of melancholy, material details, and what I might call "a loyal lightening around the eyes." I disappear and let go the light.

SOME SOURCES

After frottage there is collage.
~ Lauren Fairbanks

JANE EYRE: In his poem "An African Elegy," Robert Duncan writes:

I see her in willows, in fog, at the river of sound
in the trees.

. . . .

    And I see
all our tortures absolved in the fog,
dispersed in Death's forests, forgotten.

20C PASTORAL uses material from a Louis-Ferdinand Céline text as reproduced on a collage given to me by a friend.

LANDSCAPES uses material from two Katherine Mansfield stories.

S&M was inspired, in part, by the following lines from Sappho:

as I look at you my voice
is empty and

can say nothing as my tongue
cracks and slender fire is quick
under my skin.

        and:

                So come, darling,

with your beauty that maddens us,
and you, Praxinoa, roast the nuts
for our breakfast.

(translated by Willis Barnstone)

EVERYBODY'S AUTOBIOGRAPHY, OR NINE ATTEMPTS AT A LIFE uses material from *Revolution of the Word,* edited by Jerome Rothenberg, such as the following from Louis Zukofsky's "A"1:

Dead century, where are your motley
Country people in Leipzig.

ALICE JAMES: "about this time [...] along the shaded walk" very closely resembles a passage in entomologist E.O. Wilson's *Naturalist.* See also John Graham's *Untitled (study for La Donna Ferita),* crayon and pencil on yellowed tracing paper, which can be viewed in The Art Institute of Chicago and also, incidentally, on the cover of Diane Williams' *Excitability.*

TWO STRANGE STORIES: In Robert Walser's "Two Strange Stories," the two stories are "The Man with the Pumpkin Head" and "The Maid." The version of "Two Strange Stories" appearing in this book uses material from Diane Williams' *Excitability* and Gertrude Stein's *Ida.*

A ROOM WITH A CORPSE uses material from Ann Quin's *Berg* and Ann Radcliffe's *The Italian.*

MARY CARMICHAEL is a fictional would-be novelist in Virginia Woolf's *A Room of One's Own* about whom Woolf writes: "I am almost sure, I said to myself, that Mary Carmichael is playing a trick on us. For I feel as one feels on a switchback railway when the car, instead of sinking, as one had been led to expect, swerves up again."

SPRUNG uses material from William Carlos Williams'
"Spring and All."

ACKNOWLEDGEMENTS

Grateful acknowledgement is made to the editors who first published pieces of *Attempts at a Life* in *NOON, 5_Trope, Octopus, 3rd bed, Tarpaulin Sky, Fence, Double Room, Marginalia, Joyful Noise: an anthology of American spiritual poetry* (Autumn House Press), and *Parakeet.*

Thank you to Lisa, Sara, Beth, Diane, Bin, Laird, Rikki, Elena, and Christian.

Endless thanks to Marty.

DANIELLE DUTTON was born in Visalia, California in 1975. She is the author of a novel, *S P R A W L* (forthcoming from Clear Cut Press), and her work has appeared in various journals. She lives with her husband in Colorado where she is completing a Ph.D. in English and Creative Writing at the University of Denver.

TARPAULIN SKY PRESS
CURRENT AND FORTHCOMING TITLES

[one love affair]*, by Jenny Boully
Perfectbound & handbound editions

32 Pedals and 47 Stops, by Sandy Florian
Chapbook

Nylund, the Sarcographer, by Joyelle McSweeney
Perfectbound & handbound editions

Give Up, by Andrew Michael Roberts
Chapbook

A Mirror to Shatter the Hammer, by Chad Sweeney
Chapbook

The Pictures, by Max Winter
Perfectbound & handbound editions

www.tarpaulinsky.com